50 SCIENCE EXPERIMENTS I CAN DO

Written By Susannah Brin
And Nancy Sundquist
Illustrated By Neal Yamamoto

PRICE STERN SLOAN
Los Angeles

ISBN 0-8431-1867-9

Paper Logs

Many scientists today are worried about waste. They think people throw too many things away. They wish people would find new uses for their trash.

Burning paper logs is one way of putting old newspapers to new use. It's also a way of saving our trees! Making paper logs is easy.

You Will Need:
- water
- small tub
- old newspapers
- heavy string
- pine cones or wood chips, for wood smell (optional)

Directions:
Fill your tub with water and pine cones or wood chips. Stack up two or three sections of newspaper together. Roll them tightly into logs. Tie each log with a double knot. Do not tie your logs too tightly because they will swell with water.

Soak the logs for a few weeks. Turn them often. After you remove them from the water, set them in a sheltered area to let them dry completely. Your logs will be ready to burn in a week or so.

If you don't have a fireplace, *sell* your logs to someone who does!

Design A Glider

Carefully follow the illustrated steps below. Work on a table surface that is free from clutter. Make your folds very straight and press them down hard. If you make a mistake, don't worry. You can always start over.

You Will Need:
- heavy paper, cut 5" × 9"
- scissors
- glue or cellophane tape

Directions:
1. Fold up on center dotted line.
2. Open and fold over as shown above.
3. Fold back as shown above.
4. Fold over as shown.
5. Trim off the part that goes beyond the center line. This part is shown here by a second dotted line. Repeat steps 1-4 on other half of paper. For good balance, make sure your folds on both halves match.
6. Fold both halves down on center line.
7. Fold both sides up.
8. Glue or tape the loose folds together. These folds mark the belly of your plane. This is where you will grip it.
9. Aim plane at sky and throw!

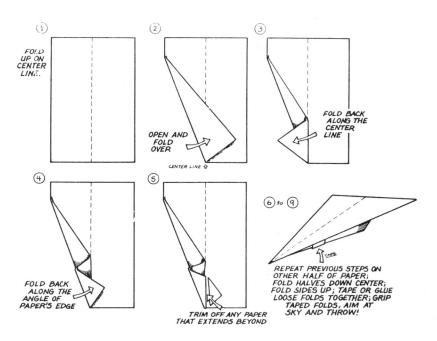

Make Your Own Soap

What if there was no such thing as bars of soap? What if you only had sudsy foam to wash with? Scientists often experiment with chemicals to find ways to make and improve products. Try this experiment to see if you can make a bar of soap.

You Will Need:
- pure laundry soap flakes (Ivory Flakes® Detergent works well)
- salt
- hot water
- large glass
- measuring cup
- tablespoon

Directions:
Put one cup of hot tap water in a measuring cup. Add five tablespoons of laundry detergent. Stir the detergent until it dissolves. Pour the detergent water into the large glass.

Fill the measuring cup again with one cup hot tap water. Add four tablespoons of salt to the water in the measuring cup. Stir the water until the salt is dissolved. Pour the salt water into the large glass on top of the soap water. Do not stir the mixture in the glass. Wait a few minutes and you will see the soap rise to the top of the water. You now have a bar of soap.

Why?
Why did the soap harden when you added the salt? The chemicals in the salt interacted with the soap molecules which made them harden. This process is the same one people use to make the bars of soap you use every day. People who make soap usually add perfume and coloring to their soap. How could you color your soap? Experiment with drops of food coloring. How can you make it smell nice?

Make Your Own Butter

What is butter? Butter is a fat. Is there fat in cream? Do the following experiment to find out.

You Will Need:
- a carton of whipping cream
- egg beater (if you use an electric one, make sure an adult is with you)
- bowl

Directions:
Pour the cream into a bowl. Whip the cream with an egg beater until it begins to harden. It will take a long time to whip the cream into butter, so don't give up. After a few minutes of whipping the cream, you will have a hard lump of butter.

Why?
Why did the cream harden into butter? Cream is the fat from milk. When you whip the cream, the fat sticks together to form butter. How does it taste? The butter that you buy in the store is made the same way except that they add a little salt and coloring. Repeat the experiment but this time add one teaspoon of honey to the cream. What does the honey add to the taste?

Turn Bones Into Rubber

This is a fun experiment and easy to do.

You Will Need:
- chicken wishbone
- chicken leg bone
- vinegar
- large jar

Directions:
Make sure the bones are not broken. Place them in a jar. Pour vinegar into the jar until the bones are completely covered. Leave the bones in the vinegar for two days.

When you take the bones out of the vinegar, they will be rubbery. Fool your friends by asking them to make a wish on your wishbone. They won't be able to break it. The wishbone will bend.

Why?
Why did the bones turn to rubber? Bones are made up of lots of calcium. Your teeth have lots of calcium in them, too. Calcium is very hard. The vinegar dissolved the calcium in the bones. Without the calcium, the bones became rubbery. Find out what foods contain calcium.

Crystal Garden

A crystal is a three-dimensional structure that repeats itself. Rocks are crystals. Rock candy is made of large sugar crystals. Each grain of sand is a crystal of quartz rock with the edges worn away. You can learn how crystals are formed by making a crystal garden.

You Will Need:
- old pie plate
- an assortment of rocks
- water
- salt
- food coloring
- measuring cup
- tablespoon

Directions:
Arrange your rocks in the old pie plate. Fill a measuring cup with ¼ cup of hot tap water. Add two tablespoons of salt to the water. Stir the water and salt until the salt dissolves. Add two or three drops of blue food coloring to the salt water. Stir the mixture. Pour your blue solution over the rocks in the pie plate.

Place your rock garden in the sun. In a day or two the water will evaporate, leaving blue crystals.

Why?
Why did crystals form on the rocks and on the plate? Salt is a crystal. When the water evaporated the salt returned to its natural crystal form. As more water evaporated more salt crystals formed on top of the other salt crystals. If you place your rock garden in a shady spot, the water will evaporate slowly. The slower the water evaporates the larger the crystals will be. Repeat the experiment using different amounts of salt, water and colors. Try the experiment using epsom salts. Are the epsom salt crystals different from the salt crystals?

Bubble Chains And Double Bubbles

Blowing bubbles is fun. Did you know that a soap bubble is one of the thinnest things that can be seen without the use of a microscope? Soap bubbles are just thin puffs of air surrounded by a watery film.

You Will Need:
- different sizes of cans (open at both ends)
- paper cup
- drinking straw
- plastic funnel
- cake pan
- dishwashing detergent (dry powder)
- tablespoon

Directions:
Put eight tablespoons of dishwashing detergent in a cake pan or other flat-bottomed pan. Add a little bit of warm water. Mix the water and soap solution gently. You want to make a thin, but not sudsy, solution.

Dip a can into the solution. Blow gently through the can to make the soap film stretch out. When you have a round or oval bubble, twist the can to close and release the bubble into the air. The larger the can, the larger the bubble you can make.

Make double bubbles and bubble chains. To make a bubble chain, dip the tin can into the solution and blow a bubble. Before releasing the bubble, turn the can upside down so that the bubble is facing the floor. Dip a drinking straw into the soap solution. Carefully place the tip of the straw into the bottom of the bubble on the can. Blow gently. Repeat to make a whole chain of bubbles.

Experiment with different objects to blow bubbles. Just remember that bubbles break when they touch something dry. Always make sure that your bubble blower is wet.

The Ocean In A Bottle

Which is heavier, water or oil? Can you mix water and oil?

You Will Need:
- tall, thin bottle with a cap
- vegetable oil
- water
- blue food coloring

Directions:
Fill the bottle half full of water. Add a drop of blue food coloring. Fill the jar to the very top with the oil. Don't leave room for air at the top of the jar. Screw the cap on as tight as you can.

Place the jar on the table and roll it gently back and forth. The blue water will move back and forwards just like the ocean waves. Now shake the jar. Little bubbles form just as they do when the ocean is stormy.

Why?
Why didn't the oil and water mix? Some chemicals won't mix together. When chemicals won't mix, scientists say that the two chemicals are not attracted to each other. Why did the water stay on the bottom? Water is heavier than oil. When you rolled the jar back and forth, the water moved against the oil on the top.

Experiment to find what other chemicals won't mix with oil. Try oil and salt. Test hand lotion and water or furniture polish and water. Is there oil in hand lotion and furniture polish? What happens when you mix oil and milk?

Rock Hound

Geology is a science that studies the beginning of the earth, its history and its structure. One way geologists learn more about the earth is by collecting then studying rocks. You can learn more about where you live by collecting rocks and studying them.

You Will Need:
- notebook
- pencil
- adhesive tape
- newspaper
- gloves and backpack
- soap & old toothbrush

Directions:
Begin by looking around your neighborhood. If you live in the country, you can find rocks in the fields, near streams and even in your backyard. If you live in the city, begin by looking at the buildings. Most of the rocks used in buildings came from the earth such as granite, marble, slate, sandstone and limestone. You can't chip a piece of rock off a building but you can find broken bits of rocks where buildings are being torn down.

When you find a rock for your collection, label the rock with the white tape. If it is your first rock, write the numeral 1 on the label. Now write 1 in your notebook. Next to it write the date and the exact spot where you found the rock. Then write the name of the rock. (You can fill in the name of the rock later, if you don't know it.) Wrap the rock in newspaper and put it in your backpack.

At home, wash your rocks with soapy water and an old toothbrush. Dry your rocks and add them to your collection.

You can find books in your library to help you identity the rocks you find. As you learn more about rocks, you will probably want to arrange your collection by how they are formed or by the minerals in the rock.

Leaf Prints

You can collect leaves and make prints of them. Botanists collect leaves from trees so that they can study the life of plants.

You Will Need:
- leaves (fresh, not dried)
- newspaper & white paper
- inkpad
- tweezers
- scissors

Directions:
Cut the newspaper into squares a little bigger than the leaf. Carefully lay your leaf, underside down, on the inkpad. Put one of the newspaper squares over the leaf on the inkpad.

Gently run your finger over the newspaper and leaf. Be sure to press the leaf into the ink evenly. Carefully lift off the newspaper. Using the tweezers, lift the leaf from the inkpad. Place the inked side of the leaf on a piece of white paper. Using a clean piece of newspaper, press the inky leaf onto the white paper. Press evenly along the leaf outline.

Remove the newspaper from the leaf. Lift the leaf from the white paper with tweezers. Wait for the ink to dry, then label your leaf print.

The leaves of a tree can reveal a lot about the tree. Did you discover any secrets about the tree from the leaf?

Bark Bark

How can you identify a tree? One way is by the bark. You can learn about trees by making bark rubbings. Bark rubbings are fun to make and they don't hurt the tree.

You Will Need:
- white paper
- adhesive tape
- large crayon
- pen or pencil

Directions:
Pick a tree. Tape your paper to the tree. Using the side of a large crayon, rub up and down on the paper against the tree. When you have finished your rubbing, remove the paper and tape from the tree. Label your rubbing with the name of the tree.

Do another bark rubbing from a different tree. Do the rubbings look alike? How are they different? Which trees have thick bark? Which trees are smooth? Make a bark rubbing collection.

Save A Spider Web

Spiders spin beautiful webs to trap insects. (Spiders aren't insects.) First, the spider makes long threads that it attaches to a wall or object. These long threads run from the object to the center of the web. After attaching the web, the spider spins a beautiful design. The sticky design traps insects. You can preserve a spider web. Here's how!

You Will Need:
• colored construction paper
• white or light-colored spray paint
• scissors

Directions:
Find a spider web outside in a tree or low bush. Make sure that the spider is not in the web. If you see the spider, frighten it away with a little stick, but don't harm the spider.

Stand a few feet from the web. Starting at the top of the web, spray a fine mist of paint over the entire web. Don't overspray because too much paint can break the web.

Before the paint dries, place a dark piece of paper on the web. Press the paper gently on the web. Hold the paper very still and cut the guy lines of the web (see picture).

Slowly lower your paper to the ground. The web should stick to the paper. Let it dry, then label it.

Fake Fossils

Fossils are imprints of dead plants and animals that were preserved long ago in the earth's crust. If you make some fake fossils, you will discover how real fossils are made.

You Will Need:
- small seashell
- two small round plastic containers
- old spoon
- water
- plaster of Paris
- petroleum jelly (such as Vaseline®)

Directions:
Fill one container half full of plaster of Paris. Slowly, add water and stir until the plaster is thick and creamy.

Cover small seashells with petroleum jelly. Press the shells in the plaster. Press the shells until the plaster rises to the top of the sides of the shell. Don't let the plaster cover the shell. Let the shells dry in the plaster overnight.

In the morning, pull the shells out of the plaster. You will see imprints of shells. The imprints of the shell in the plaster are fake fossils. Your fossil took only one day to make. Real fossils are formed over million of years!

Coat the shell imprint in the plaster with petroleum jelly. Mix up another batch of plaster in the other container. Pour the plaster into the shell imprints. Wait one day, then carefully pry out the plaster from the imprints. You have just made plaster copies of your shells.

Try making fake fossils with dried flowers, leaves, nuts and dead insects. Sometimes you can find real fossils in dry riverbeds or imprinted on rocks.

Growing Beans On Cotton

The process of growing plants from seeds is fun to watch. Try the following experiment to discover how a plant grows from a seed.

You Will Need:
- lima beans, navy beans, lentils
- cotton balls
- jar
- water

Directions:

Fill the jar with water. Make a ring of cotton around the top of the jar. Sprinkle water on the cotton. Place the beans on the cotton in a circle around the jar. Put the jar with the beans in a warm, sunny spot.

All plants need water and air. While the beans are growing be sure to keep water in the jar. Don't overwater. In a week, the beans should begin to crack open and send out little roots.

Try the experiment using melon seeds, tomato seeds or fruit seeds.

Why?

Why do the seeds disappear as the new plant grows? Seeds contain the beginnings of new plants. The seed will crack open and a sprout will appear. As the sprout reaches toward the sun, roots will begin to grow downwards. Roots help the plant stand upright. The seed covering drops off and dries up.

Mold Jar Gardens

Molds are really plants called fungi. You can grow several types of molds with food from your kitchen.

You Will Need:
- jars with lids
- slice of bread
- apple, orange, banana with bruises on the skin
- water

Directions:
Find a dusty place on the floor. Use the slice of bread to wipe up the dust. (If there is no dust, leave the bread in the air for an hour.) Sprinkle the dusty bread with water and put it in the jar. Close the lid of the jar tightly. The bread will smell bad while the mold is growing. Put the jar in a warm, dark cupboard for one week.

Put an apple, orange or banana in a jar. Tighten the lid. It is best to use fruit that is bruised or already old. Place the jar in a dark cupboard for one week.

Check your mold jars. What does the mold look like on the bread? Is the bread mold different from the mold on the fruit? Are the molds different colors?

Why?
Why didn't the mold need sunlight to grow? Mold is a plant that does not need sunlight for its food. Mold gets its food from the organic material on which it lives. In this experiment the food source for the mold was bread and fruit. Repeat the experiment, but this time put the jars in the refrigerator. How long does it take mold to grow in the cold?

Pinwheel Air Detector

Did you know that air is always moving? Air moves up, down, left and right. The movement of air is called currents. You can make a pinwheel to help you detect which way the air is moving.

You Will Need:
- notebook paper
- pencil
- scissors
- pin

Directions:
Fold the piece of notebook paper in half, then in half again. Crease the fold by running your fingernail along the edge. Open the paper. Cut along each fold almost to the center. Using the pin, pin every other point to the center (see picture). Push the pin with the paper into the eraser of the pencil. You now have a pinwheel.

With your pinwheel air detector you can find air currents that move in different directions. Which way does the air move when you hold the pinwheel over a lamp? Which way does the air move if you hold the pinwheel near the bottom of an open refrigerator door? Hold the pinwheel in the wind. Which way is the wind blowing?

Why?
Why did the pinwheel move in different directions? The movement of air is affected by temperature. The air by the lamp is warm. Warm air rises. The air coming out of the refrigerator is cold. Cold air moves down. When the cold air from the refrigerator warms, what will happen?

Dried-Flower Machine

You can save flowers by pressing them in a book. But if you would like to keep a whole arrangement of flowers, you need to dry them. Flowers lose their colors when they die. This experiment will show you how to keep the colors in the flowers.

You Will Need:
- borax
- white sand
- fresh flowers
- shoe box
- scissors
- measuring cup

Directions:
Pick some flowers with stems. Mix four cups of borax with five cups of white sand. Pour a layer of sand mixture on the bottom of the shoebox. Carefully place each flower, head down, in the sand. Add more sand mixture until the head of the flower and the leaves are covered. Put the lid on the box. Leave your shoebox in a dark place for 10 days.

Gently, remove each flower. The flowers will be dry, so handle carefully. Did your flowers stay the same colors?

Why?
Why did the flowers keep their colors? The borax and sand mixture helped pull the moisture from the flowers quickly. By drying quickly, the flowers should not lose their shapes or colors.

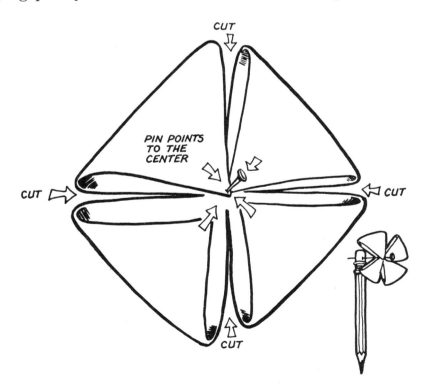

CUT

PIN POINTS TO THE CENTER

CUT

CUT

CUT

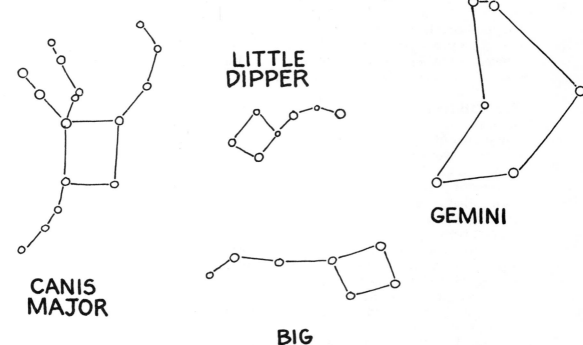

LITTLE DIPPER

GEMINI

CANIS MAJOR

BIG DIPPER

Star Projector

Stars make pictures in the sky at night. If you go to a planetarium, you will see a model of the stars and planets projected on the ceiling. Make your own planetarium with this star projector.

You Will Need:
- large sheets of heavy paper
- grocery box
- tape
- pencil
- scissors
- flashlight

Directions:
Cut off the lid and back of the box. Your box should resemble a pen with no top or floor. Copy the star pictures on this page on a sheet of paper. The paper should cover one of the openings on the box. Tape your star paper to the open top.

Turn off all the lights in the room. Place a flashlight inside the box. Turn on the flashlight. The light should shine through the star openings. The star patterns will be projected on the ceiling. This works best when the room is very dark.

Why?
Why can't we see stars during the day? The sun is a star and its brightness hides the other stars. Turn on the lights in the room. Can you still see your stars projected on the calling? Why not?

Sun Power

We all know that the sun gives off heat. But did you know that you could cook with sun power? Instead of boiling water for tea on the stove, try this experiment.

You Will Need:
- four tea bags
- two large jars with lids
- cold water

Directions:
Fill each jar with water. Put two teabags in each jar. Holding the teabags with labels, lower them into the water. Fold the labels over the outside rim of the jars. Put the lids on the jars. Set one jar of water in the hot sun. Put the other jar in a dark place. Wait several hours.

What color is the water in the sun? What color is the water in the jar that was in the dark?

Why?
Why was the tea water darker when left in the sun? The sun gives off heat. Tea contains chemicals that dissolve quicker in hot water than in cold water. The tea in the sun dissolved more because of the heat from the sun. Which tea tastes better? The one cooked in the sun or the one left in the dark?

Make Your Own Ant Farm

Ants live and work together in a society called a colony. Make an ant colony and see the ants build tunnels, mazes and rooms.

You Will Need:
- large glass jar with lid
- small glass jar
- loose dirt
- sugar
- water
- teaspoon
- old can

Directions:
Place the small jar upside down inside the large jar. Fill the space between the two jars with dirt. You are now ready to find some ants. Look for ants in the yard, in loose dirt in the garden or at the base of trees.

After finding some ants, you need to make an ant trap. Mix two teaspoons of sugar with a little water. You want the sugar mixture to be thick. Pour the sugar water in a line on the inside of your can. Lay the can on its side near the ants. Try to catch fifteen to twenty ants. Don't overcrowd your ant farm. Put your ants into the glass jar with the dirt. Cover the jar with a lid. Don't worry that the ants won't have air. They will get air when you feed them.

Once a week, feed your ants with a little sugar water or bird seed. Don't overfeed your ants. Now set your ant farm in a cool place. Don't disturb your ant farm for a few days. Watch as the ants build tunnels and rooms in the dirt.

Why?
Why do some ants seem to do different jobs than others? Ants are organized into groups of individuals who perform different duties. In an ant colony, there is one queen ant and many workers. The worker ants have many special jobs to do.

Flower Power

Are flowers and plants strong? Do this experiment to see flowers flex their muscles.

You Will Need:
- ten sunflower seeds
- six-inch high flower pots
- soil
- water
- piece of glass or clear plastic

Directions:
Plant the sunflower seeds in the flowerpot with dirt. Water the seeds. Don't overwater. Place the flowerpot in a warm, sunny spot. Water whenever the soil dries out.

In a few days the seeds will sprout. Before the little plants rise above the rim of the flowerpot, place a piece of glass or clear plastic over the top of the pot. The glass or plastic should be bigger than the top of the pot. Wait a few days. The little plants will lift the glass off the top of the pot.

Why?
Why did the sunflower plants lift the glass off the pot? Plants and flowers have muscle power. First, the plant pushed its way up through the dirt then it lifted the glass. Like you, plants become stronger and more powerful as they grow.

Magnet Power

Magnets have pulling power. They are usually made of iron, a common metal. Iron is made up of tiny, tiny iron atoms. Each iron atom has a tiny bit of pulling power. Do all iron objects have the pulling power of a magnet? Let's find out.

You Will Need:
- any piece of metal except a magnet
- magnet
- paper clips
- tacks & pins
- soda can
- coins
- piece of wood
- paper

Directions:
Place all of your objects on the table. Take the piece of metal and place it next to each object. Can the metal piece pick up the paper clips or anything on the table? Now use the magnet. What does the magnet pick up?

Why?
Why does the magnet have pulling power and the piece of metal doesn't? The iron atoms in metal are all going in different directions. When a magnet is made the iron atoms are all forced to go in one direction so that they have pulling power.

Try putting two magnets together. What happens? Tie a piece of string around your magnet. Fill a glass with water and put tacks, pins, and clips in the water. Use your magnet to fish out the objects. Make a chain of paper clips. How many clips can your magnet pull?

Follow The Traveling Water

Water travels up from the roots of plants, through the stems to the leaves.

You Will Need:
- two glasses of water
- a daffodil, daisy or carnation
- one long piece of celery
- blue food coloring

Directions:
Put a drop of blue food coloring in each glass of water. Put the flower in one glass and the celery stalk in the other. Be sure the flower petals and celery leaves are not touching the water. Leave the two glasses in a warm place for awhile. What happens after an hour? After a day?

Why?
Plants and vegetables have little cells filled with water. The food coloring filled the cells with color so that you could see the path water takes as it travels from the root to the flower and leaves. Look at the bottom of the celery. Can you see the little paths outlined in blue?

Foaming Exploding Volcano

You can use your homemade chemistry set to create a foaming volcano.

You Will Need:
- empty soda pop bottle
- caps from old soda pop bottles
- vinegar
- baking soda

Directions:
Fill the soda pop bottle half full with vinegar. Add a teaspoon of baking soda. Quickly press a cap down on the top of the bottle. The mixture will foam over the top as you are pressing the cap on the bottle. Step back and watch as the foaming liquid pops the top off your bottle. Try replacing the cap again. What happens if you give the bottle a little shake?

Why?
Why does the top pop off the bottle? Vinegar is an acid. Acid and baking soda mixed together form a gas called carbon dioxide. The gas pops the top off because there isn't room in the bottle for all the gas created. What other acids could you mix with baking soda to create carbon dioxide? Experiment with fruit juice, milk and water. Which one is acid?

23

Make Your Own Chemistry Set

You can make your own chemistry set with things around the house. Chemistry sets are fun and helpful in doing experiments.

You Will Need:
- small bottle with eye dropper (use an empty nosedrop bottle)
- measuring spoons & old spoons
- old clear plastic pill bottles with snap-on tops (get the bottles in different sizes – you can buy new ones at the drugstore)
- ten or twelve small baby food jars with lids
- white tape or white labels
- pen
- a box large enough to hold the contents of your chemistry set

Directions:
Put labels or white tape on each baby food jar. Now you are ready to fill your baby food jars with your chemicals. Ask your mom or dad for the following: baking soda, flour, salt, cornstarch, white vinegar, cooking oil, liquid dish soap, sugar and water. Put each item in a baby food jar and label the jar.

Label the box for your chemistry set. Put everything you have collected into the box. You will also need paper napkins, cotton balls, small drinking glass and old tin pie plates.

You can do lots of fun experiments with your chemistry set. Chemists work in laboratories where they experiment with chemicals. Sometimes chemistry experiments are messy. Make sure that your laboratory is a place that is easy to clean up.

Make Your Own Soda Pop

Orange and grape soda are easy to make. If you want to make cola you will have to experiment. First, let's make orange or grape soda.

You Will Need:
- orange or grape juice
- baking soda
- water
- drinking glasses
- measuring spoon

Cola:
- vanilla extract
- sugar
- cinnamon
- lime or lemon juice
- water
- baking soda

Directions:
Fill the drinking glass half full of water. Now add orange or grape juice to the water. Fill the glass almost full. Stir in ½ teaspoon of baking soda. The baking soda mixes with the acid of the fruit juice to make carbon dioxide. Carbon dioxide is the same gas that is used in soda pop.

Now let's make cola. The recipe for Coca-Cola® is a well-kept secret; you will have to experiment to discover the secret recipe, or at least something similar.

Directions: (Cola)
Fill a glass half full of water. Add three tablespoons of sugar, a half teaspoon of vanilla extract, a pinch of cinnamon, a half teaspoon of lemon or lime juice and a teaspoon of baking soda. Stir the mixture. Your cola will not be brown like the kind you buy in the store. Does it taste like cola? Does it need more sugar? Less sugar? Try repeating the experiment using different amounts of the juice, sugar, vanilla and cinnamon. Write down the amount of ingredients that you use. Did you discover the secret recipe?

By keeping notes of what you do you will be able to repeat the recipe which tastes the most like cola. Maybe you'll invent your own secret cola recipe!

Tin-Can Telephone Tests

There are many ways to make toy telephones. Some are better than others, but all are better than shouting. See which one works best for you.

You Will Need:
- different kinds of long string and wire
- several sizes of tin cans and stiff paper coffee cups (two of each)
- tape
- buttons, metal washers, paper clips
- notepad and pencil

Directions:
Start by making one set of phones. Ask an adult to help make a small hole in the bottoms of two tin cans. Pull the end of a long piece of string through one can hole. Tie a button to the string. Do the same to the other can. The buttons will keep the string from pulling out.

Try your phone out with someone make other end. Walk far enough apart that you can't hear each other talk using normal voices.

Now conduct your tests. But before you begin, think about this question: How can your assistant always have the same loudness of voice from test to test? It'll be difficult. Instead of speaking, you might have him or her hold the can next to a radio, stereo or loud clock.

Once you've tested the phone you've made, you might want to make several different phones at once. That way you can listen to one right after the other. They'll be easier to compare than if you had to wait between each test to make another phone.

Many different things can change the loudness of the sounds your phones carry. Some of them will be difficult to record. For example, how can you tell you're holding the string just as tight in all tests? If you were in a science laboratory, you would have special instruments to help you measure these changes from test to test. However, you can still make some interesting discoveries. Just keep your eyes – and your *ears* – wide open!

Tests:
Pull string tight.

Let string hang loose.

Replace string with fishing line or other kinds of wire. Try other kinds of string and heavy thread.

Replace the buttons with knots, tape, paper clips, metal washers.

Add another hole to the bottom of the can and tie the string through the holes.

Try different sizes of cans.

Try stiff-paper coffee cups (the kind with handles, so your fingers won't muffle the sound).

Seeing Red

Do you believe that you could look at red and see blue? Well, seeing is believing!

You Will Need:
• sheet of red paper
• sheet of white paper

Directions:
Stare at the red paper for about sixty seconds. Now look at the white paper. Does it look blue-green? This is called *after-image*.

There are six basic colors in the color *spectrum*. See if other colors have after-images. Make a chart to record your findings.

Spectrum	After-image
red	blue-green
orange	
yellow	
green	
blue	
violet	

Why?
After staring at the red paper, your eyes got tired. They could no longer see red. White paper, like sunlight, is white because it reflects all the colors in the spectrum, including red. But when your eyes got tired, they couldn't see any of the red colors in the white paper. All they could see was the other end of the spectrum – blue-green!

The Street Where You Live

You can find full-page maps of the stars, of the world, of the United States and even of your city. But you'll probably never find a map of the place you know best of all – the street where you live – unless you make one!

You Will Need:
• paper
• colored pencils or crayons
• ruler

Directions:
Maps tell a lot with hardly any words at all. They are like pictures. Before you begin to make you map, think about what you want to put in it. Do you want to show the homes or buildings on *both* sides of your street? The backyards on both sides? The backyards *behind* these backyards? Do you want to show the streets at both ends of your block? You may have to start your map more than once to figure out how to squeeze everything in. It'll help if you draw the streets first.

Once you've drawn in your streets, write their names between the lines. Be sure you get their spellings right!

Now put in anything that's in any of the backyards. Remember that you'll be drawing the tops of trees, gardens, dog pens, pools and sand boxes. Some things, such as fences, don't really have tops that look like anything. Think of a way to draw them so they do.

When you're finished with your map, think of other favorite places you'd like to map out. City parks, amusement parks, swimming pools, schools and downtown all make good maps. Save the maps you make and collect them in a book. Someday you might move. Your maps will help you remember where you once lived and the things you used to do.

Balloon "Moon Rockets"

If the earth were a balloon, could it fly to the moon? You can't find out the answer to this question, but you *can* find out how far much smaller balloons can fly.

You Will Need:
- about 50 feet of very thin wire (fishline will do)
- several balloons of various sizes (small, medium, large) and shapes (oblong, round, heart, etc.)
- tape
- plastic straws
- red pen
- ruler
- notepad

Directions:
First mark off every five feet of the wire with red ink so you can later measure flight distances. Then tie one end of the wire inside a second-story window. Let the other end hang free outside the window, touching the ground. Thread a straw through this end of the wire.

Decide which balloon you want to test first. On a pad of paper, note its size and shape. At this point, it would be good if you could get a friend to help.

Blow up the balloon. While holding its mouth tight, tape the balloon to the straw. (For extra long balloons, try using two straws.) Now you're ready for blast-off.

Pull the wire tight and hold the balloon close to the ground. Release the balloon and watch for the last red mark it passes. Record the number of feet it flies. If you have two balloons of the same kind, try taping one beneath the other. Now you have dual rockets! Take all your balloons on a test flight. Decide which size and shape is best for air travel . . . If the earth were a balloon, would its shape make a good rockets?

Bringing In The Rain

You never learn how much rain falls in your own backyard from your local weather reports. That's because each report gives the average amount of rain that has fallen throughout your city. The next time it rains, do the measuring yourself. Compare your findings with the TV weather reporter.

You Will Need:
- coffee can
- funnel as wide as your coffee can
- tall, thin bottle with straight sides (Try an empty pill container or visit a science or farm supply store.)
- measuring tape
- paper tape and pen or paint and fine-line brush

Directions:

A large jar is best for trapping raindrops. But the rain it collects is difficult to measure if rainfall has been light. You can solve this problem by using a smaller bottle for measurement.

Mark off one inch on one side of the can. Carefully pour exactly one inch of water into it. Now pour the water into your smaller bottle. Mark off the water level. This is your new "inch." Use a ruler to mark off eight equal parts, or "fractions," on the side of the bottle. If you don't know how to use a ruler, get someone older to help you. If your bottle is tall enough, mark off another inch or two.

Wait for rain. Look for an open, flat area in your front or backyard. Find a spot that won't get extra rain dripping from trees or roofs. Set out the can with the funnel on top. The funnel will trap the raindrops that fall on its rim.

Immediately after the rain has stopped, bring in the jar. Pour the rainwater into the bottle. Read the amount to the nearest fraction or ask someone to help you read it. Now wait for the evening news. Did you get more or less rain than the rest of the city?

Note:

If you think about it, you'll realize that the wider the coffee can, the more water there'll be to the inch! How do scientists know what's a true inch of water? They have a special ruler for measuring rainfall. It's called a *rain gauge,* and it costs only a few dollars. If you're interested in seeing how it works, you can find one in a farm or science supply store. Ask your librarian to help you search for the store nearest you.

How Does Your Garden Grow?

Some people say that your garden is only as good as your soil. Do you have soil that's good for growing things? It's easy to find out.

You Will Need:
- your fingers
- water
- plastic containers (optional)

Directions:
There are three main kinds of soil. No soil is just one kind, but mixtures of all three. The best soil for gardening is not too much of one kind or another. Good soil also has lots of dead plant life in it.

Go outside and dig up some dirt. Run your fingers through it. What does it feel like? Moisten it with water. Now what does it feel like? Look at the chart below and see if you can find your soil described. If you think your soil is not very good for gardening, you can buy products that will make it good for growing almost anything.

You can collect soil from different parts of town. Just put your soil samples in plastic containers with notes saying where you found each one. The next time you go on vacation to a different area of the country, you can collect soil that is very different to add to your collection.

Mostly sandy	Feels rough to the touch. Doesn't hold together when wet. Can see tiny grains.
Mostly silt	Grains are smaller than sand grains. Feels smoother than sand. Holds together when wet and makes light smear.
Mostly clay	Feels very hard when dry and sticky when wet. Makes smooth smear when wet. Cannot see separate grains at all.

Mirror Multiplication

The question here is, "Mirror, mirror, on the wall, who's the most beautiful me of all?" You need two large mirrors for this experiment. Ask an adult to help you move the mirrors.

You Will Need:
• two large mirrors

Directions:
Lean two large mirrors against opposite walls (such as in a hallway) or against objects that are only a few feet apart. Sit down between them. How many of you (front and back) do you see?

Why?
You see yourself in a mirror because light bounces from the mirror to your eyes. You see many of you with a second mirror behind you because the light is now also bouncing back and forth between the mirrors. With each bounce, you get smaller and smaller and smaller until you seem to disappear!

The Shadow Knows

How do you measure something taller than a yardstick? Try this method out. For starters, measure your school or house.

You Will Need:
• sun
• string
• yardstick

Directions:
Wait for a sunny day. Find your school's shadow. Make another shadow with a yardstick. Mark off the length of the shadow with your string. How many times does the yardstick's shadow go into the school's shadow? Multiply the number of times by three. The answer should be the height of the school. For example, if your yardstick's shadow goes into the school's shadow 10 times, the school is about thirty feet tall.

Now look for more long shadows for measuring.

Sight Unseen!

Watch a parade from behind a crowd. Spot a friend coming up the street. Look for the arrival of the birthday girl at a surprise party. Play private eye! With a periscope, you'll be able to do all these things and more.

You Will Need:
- long cardboard box, wide enough to hold two pocket mirrors
- two pocket mirrors
- tape
- scissors
- pen
- ruler

Directions:
Draw a two-inch square toward the bottom of one side of the box. Draw another two-inch square toward the top of the opposite side. Cut the length of one edge of your box to open it up and make it easier to work with. Now cut out the square you've just drawn.

Tape a pocket mirror *below* the bottom square so that it's slanting up toward the top of the box. Tape the other mirror just *above* the top square so that it's slanting down toward the bottom. (Study the illustration carefully and match the 45° angles of the mirrors shown. Notice that the angles of the mirrors are parallel.)

Fold the box closed and test your periscope. You may have to fiddle a bit with the mirrors. When they are in place, the top mirror will "see" the object first, then "bounce" it down to the bottom mirror, which "bounces" it to your eyes. Your periscope proves that light travels in straight lines.

When you have the mirrors in the right positions, tape the box back up. Now you're ready to scope out any scene!

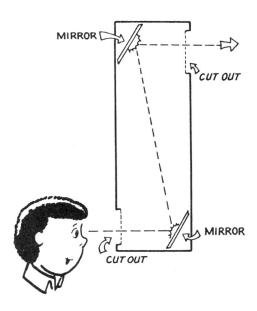

The Shadow Shows

You can make shadows just like the sun does if you have a lamp and a blank wall. All you have to do is stand between them. Try using your hands to cast shadows that look like animal heads. Your fingers will make good, pointy ears. Practice making your animals get bigger and smaller by moving your hands around.

Once you get good at making shadows, put on some shadow shows.

You Will Need:
- regular paper
- tracing paper
- animal cookie cutter
- a paper punch
- scissors
- tape
- straws or Popsicle® sticks
- flashlight or table lamp

Directions:
Place the cookie cutters on the paper. Trace around them. Cut out your animals. Make eyes using your paper punch. Tape the animals to straws or sticks.

If you don't have a box to make a stage, you can begin rehearsal now. Just gather your shadow puppets and your shadow puppeteers, turn on the light and begin making up stories. Your puppets will act your stories out, and you will be their voices.

If you want to make a shadow box, read on. Find a medium-sized cardboard box. Get someone older to help you cut off the flaps and the bottom. Tape tracing paper where the bottom used to be. Tape against the inside of the box. The paper is your screen, or your "wall."

Put your shadow box on a table. Shine a light behind it. Bring on the shadow puppets. Your performance is ready to begin!

Hairy Eggheads

Many plants grow quite easily. Here's a fun way of watching them.

You Will Need:
- eggshell half
- dirt
- felt-tip pen
- watercress, grass, or parsley seeds

Directions:
Do you know what watercress is? It looks a little like grass, but tastes a whole lot better. Many people like to use it in sandwiches, salads and egg dishes. If you plant watercress seeds, your eggshell garden will be fun, but useful too.

Clean out half an eggshell. If it has been hard-boiled, chip off the top. Then scoop out the bottom with a spoon. Gently run water over it and let it dry.

Draw a face on the eggshell with a felt-tip pen. Fill it with dirt and sprinkle seed on top. Press them down lightly. Moisten the dirt every day or whenever it dries out. Soon your egghead will sprout "hairs" that stand straight up on their ends.

A Cagey Contraption

When you're studying insects, you want them to feel comfortable. That way, they'll behave just as they do in their own "homes." Jars with holes in the lid are OK, but nothing like the great outdoors.

Insects are cramped, cold, and suffocating in jars. Homemade wire insect cages are good because they let breezes blow through. They're easy to work with. You can even make a mini-woods in there. If you build your cage with care, it will be a home away from home for any insect you snare!

You Will Need:
- plaster of Paris
- two aluminum pie pans
- wire mesh (such as the mesh used for window screens; make sure the holes in the mesh are small so the insects don't fall through!)

Directions:
Pour a layer of plaster of Paris into one pie pan. Roll the wire mesh into a tube and set it down inside the pan. Let the plaster harden. Use the second pie pan as your top, to be lifted on and off as needed.

Now you are ready to collect your insects. Notice the plants you find them in. Bring them home, too. These plants are probably what your insects like for food and/or shelter.

In the fall, look for caterpillars. Soon they'll start spinning their cocoons. If you find some cocoons, leave them outside for the winter or put them in your refrigerator. If you leave them in your house, the heat will make them think it's spring in December. Then butterflies and moths will appear, and there won't be any food for them to eat.

In the spring, begin sprinkling the cocoons with water every week. When your butterflies emerge, give them fresh leaves to eat. After you have finish your study, be sure to set your captives free!

Make Your Own Animated Movies!

First there were photographs, and then there were movies. The people who invented movies made an important discovery. They took many photographs of one thing that was slightly different in each photograph. Then the inventors viewed the photographs rapidly, one after the other. The object in the pictures appeared to be moving! This discovery was the first step; the invention was the second. The invention they made was the motion picture camera!

You can't make a motion picture camera at home, but you can make motion pictures! Here's how.

You Will Need:
- fourteen or more small blank cards (index cards will do)
- pen

Directions:
Practice by drawing a simple cartoon.

On the top card, draw the side view of a man standing in front of a chair, about to sit down. Just use stick figures for now. Make your drawing on the right side of the card.

On the next card, draw the same man and chair in the same position on the card. This time draw the man so that his legs are bent just a tiny bit.

On the next card, make the man's legs bent just a little bit more.

On the next card, make the man's legs bent just a little bit more than the last two cards.

With each card, continue drawing the man's legs more and more bent until he is finally sitting down. At this point you'll probably have more cards left. Repeat the drawings in reverse, to show the man standing up.

Hold the cards together in your left hand. Now flip them from top to bottom with your right thumb. Does your man appear to be moving? He should.

Try adding more action to your cartoon. For example, you can add a card after the man has sat down. Draw another picture of him sitting down, only this time show his full face. When you flip the cards, he will appear to be turning his head to look at you!

Now make up your own cartoon show. Simply turn over the cards and draw another "movie" on the back.

Harness The Wind!

After scientists design a plane, they make a small model of it. They test this model to make sure it can fly before they spend the time and money building the real thing. They use a wind tunnel to create air currents like those the plane will meet in the sky.

The wind tunnels scientists use are much larger and more complicated than any you can make at home. However, with a dozen milk cartons, you can get a pretty good idea of how a wind tunnel works. Start saving your one-quart cartons today.

You Will Need:
• a dozen one-quart milk cartons
• tape
• scissors

Directions:
Cut off both ends of each carton. Stack them up in a rectangle three cartons high and four cartons wide. Wrap tape around them. Place your wind tunnel in front of a blowing fan.

If you have a paper plane, test it out. Thread a long piece of light-weight string through its tail. Stand in front of the wind tunnel and hold onto your plane by the string. How well does your plane fly? Does it lift up, point down or stay aimed straight ahead? Can you correct any error in your plane's design by folding (or trimming) the wings or tail differently? If you were a scientist, would you give the go-ahead to build a real plane modeled after your paper one?

A Sub In The Tub

Here's an experiment that shows how air and water can work together.

You Will Need:
- three-foot plastic tube (the kind pet stores sell for aquariums)
- large juice bottle
- washcloth

Directions:
Cut the tube into three pieces – one long and two short. Make the short ones each about six inches long. Poke the long piece into the bottle so that it touches the bottom. Let the rest of it hang out. This loose end should curl back over the end in the bottle. It marks the top of your sub.

Fold up a washcloth and push it into the mouth of the bottle. It should fit tightly. Hold the two short tubes together and squeeze them in between the washcloth and the jar on the underside of the sub. These tubes should hang out, too.

If everything's tight, you're ready for your first mission. Fill the bathtub and launch your vessel. Put the long tube in your mouth. You can probably guess what you do next. Suck air through the tube, and your sub will begin its descent. Blow air through the tube, and your sub will rise to the surface.

Why?
When you suck air through the tube, the sub replaces the air it's lost with water, and descends. When you blow air through the tube, the sub fills with air, and bubbles coming out of the short tubes force it to the surface.

The Shape Of Rain

We think of a raindrop as looking like a teardrop. Often it does when it hits a hard surface like a window pane. But falling through the sky, the raindrop is a tiny, round ball or *sphere*. If the sun is out, the raindrop becomes a *prism*. It bends the sunlight and splits it into the separate colors of the *spectrum*. Together, millions of raindrops make the rainbow we see when the sun peeps through at the end of a shower. The lower the sun, the higher the rainbow will be in the sky.

You don't have to wait for a rain shower to see a rainbow, though. You can make one of your own quite easily.

You Will Need:
- sun
- garden hose with a nozzle

Directions:
During early morning or late afternoon, turn on the garden hose. Turn the nozzle so that you have a fine spray. Point the hose away from the sun and toward a dark background (a clump of trees or a building). How many colors can you see?

Sunlight, or white light, contains all the colors of the spectrum. When water bends the light, we see the colors and call it a rainbow. There are six main colors in the spectrum: red, orange, yellow, green, blue and violet. Their order never changes. Red is the color that is bent the least so it's always on top. Violet is bent the most so it's always on the bottom. In different combinations, these six colors make up all the colors that exist.

Somewhere Over The Fogbow!

The fogbow may not be as well known as its more popular cousin, the rainbow. However, some people think the fogbow is much more beautiful. It's not hard to find one if you know where to look.

You Will Need:
- fog
- good eyesight

Directions:
Watch for an early morning fog. Wait for the sun to start peeking through. As soon as it does, rush outside. Look carefully at the tiny goblets of water in the air around you. Suddenly, you will see the fogbow. It is shaped like a rainbow, but is not as big. Except for a hazy red top and a misty blue bottom, it is almost entirely pearly white! If nothing else, you'll find the fogbow one unforgettable sight.

Note:
In the United States, we say a pot of gold rests at the end of a rainbow. But in Scotland, where mists abound, myth has it that it's only at the end of a fogbow that gold can be found.

Stop A Beetle In Its Tracks

The beetle is one of the few insects this trap will work on.

You Will Need:
- empty tuna or cat food can
- something for scooping dirt
- small piece of meat

Directions:
Look for a spot in your yard away from where people walk. Scoop out a hole in the ground as deep as your can. Set your can inside the hole. Cover the edges with grass. Drop in a small piece of meat, and go about your business. Chances are you'll find a beetle on your return. The beetle will not be able to climb, jump, fly or in any way fight its way out of this trap.

If the beetle has already eaten the meat, give it some more. Watch the way it moves its mouth. Set it free when it's had its fill.

As it scurries away, watch how it moves and where it goes. This is the spot you'll want to be the next time you want to look up a beetle!

Measure A Tree

With a little help from a friend you can measure the height of a tree.

You Will Need:
- a friend
- yardstick
- tree

Directions:
Start at the base of the tree. Walk away from the tree for eleven paces. Be sure to walk in a straight line. Ask your friend to place the yardstick upright at eleven paces. Now walk one more step past the yardstick. Lie down on your stomach facing the yardstick. Look at the yardstick, then look past the yardstick to the top of the tree.

Your eyeline will create an angle from the yardstick to the top of the tree. Read the inch number on your yardstick at the point where you made the angle to the top of the tree. For example, if your yardstick reading is twenty-seven inches, the tree is approximately twenty-seven feet tall.

Why?
Why is this method of measuring tall trees useful? Some trees are so high that you can only make approximate measurements in height.

Get To Know An Ant!

The ant is one of the most interesting insects. It's always on the go and often lugging around more food than a tractor could tow! Look in your yard for an ant to study. Take this book and the items below with you.

You Will Need:
- red nail polish
- stiff paper
- stale bread crumbs
- an old piece of cloth
- molasses

Directions:
Select your ant. Dab a tiny dot of nail polish on the back of one of its thighs. The red dot will help you tell it from the other ants.

Follow the ant's movements for a few minutes. If it strays out of sight, pick it up with your paper and set it back down where it was. Does it head back in the direction it was going? Where is it going? Why? Where is its anthill?

Does the ant move at the same speed all the time? Does it move in a straight line? What does it do when it stops?

Break off a bread crumb a little larger than the ant. Put it in the ant's path. Does the ant pick it up? What happens if you take the bread away and put it behind the ant? Does the ant find it? Or does it simply go on its way?

Try forming a ring of earth around the bread. Does the ant cross the ring to get to the food, or lose all interest?

Put a few crumbs of bread near the anthill. How many ants come running? Now put a bunch of bread crumbs down. Does this attract many more ants?

Pour some molasses on a piece of cloth. Make a scent trail by dragging the cloth along the ground near the anthill. Do the ants start moving along the trail? Try different scents. Are the ants attracted more to one scent than another?

Think of more questions to ask. Questions like these have led scientists to many important discoveries.

One last question: Where did the ant with the red dot go?

Freezer Forces

Do you think you can pop a cork without touching it? Here's one way to find out.

You Will Need:
- soda bottle
- cork
- water

Directions:
Find a cork that fits your bottle. Make sure the cork is not too tight. Fill the bottle with water. Put the cork on and set the bottle in the freezer. Wait until the end of the day to check the bottle. If the water is frozen, the cork will be gone.

Why?
As water freezes it expands, which means it takes up more space and forces the cork to "go looking for another resting place." There's less space for both the water and the cork. If the cork is on too tight, it will force the water to move, and the bottle will crack.

The Fizz-Skimper Detector

Here's a device for people who like lots of bubbles in their sodas and are sometimes disappointed by the bottled drinks they buy.

You Will Need:
- several same-size bottles of cold carbonated drinks (club soda, cola, ginger ale and orange are good to test.)
- as many same-size balloons as you have bottles
- bottle opener (if caps don't screw off)

Directions:
Ask a friend to help you with this experiment. Remove the labels from the bottles so that you can see the bubble action better. Decide which soda's bubbles you want to measure first.

Grip a balloon by its mouth and get ready to fit it over the mouth of the bottle. Ask your friend to remove the cap. Quickly stretch the balloon over the bottle.

How big does the balloon get? What's causing it to blow up? What happens when you shake the bottle gently? What happens when you squeeze the balloon?

Try another soda bottle with another balloon. How big does this balloon get? Is it bigger or smaller than the first balloon? Can you explain why?

Continue testing all your sodas. Rank them by their bubble counts. Do your tastebuds agree with your fizz-skimper detector's findings?

Why?
The bubbles in soda drinks are a gas called carbon dioxide (also called CO_2). This gas is forced into the bottled liquid under tremendous pressure at the bottling plant. Then the bottle is quickly capped.

When the buyer later uncaps the bottle, the pressure is released and forces the gas out of the bottle in the form of bubbles. When you put a balloon on top of the bottle, it traps the bubbles and stretches to make room for them. The more bubbles there are, the more the balloon will stretch. You can try to squeeze the gas back into the bottle, but it won't stay. That's because you don't have as much pressure to work with as the factory does.

Liberty Island In A Bowl

For many years, the chemicals in the air of New York harbor have been eating away at the Statue of Liberty. They are causing the metals of her body to *corrode*. With a few household items, you can easily recreate the weather of Liberty Island.

You Will Need:

- two twist-ties
- two pennies
- paper towel
- bowl
- salt
- vinegar
- plastic wrap
- rubber band
- fingernail file

Directions:

Fold a paper towel and place it in the bottom of a shallow bowl. Dampen it with water. Sprinkle on a little salt. Add a dash of vinegar.

With a fingernail file scrape the edges of your pennies to remove any dirt or coating. Remove the paper from your twist-ties and scrape the wires until they are shiny, too.

Wrap one wire around a penny. Wind up the other wire into a small coil.

Place the two pennies and the coil of wire on the paper towel. Cover the bowl with plastic wrap.

Look in on the bowl every few hours. Which of your three samples corrodes the fastest?

Why?

The salt and water on the towel duplicate the salt water spray that's always hitting Liberty. The vinegar is the acid in the air from industrial pollution. The plastic wrap helps keep the bowl humid, as if surrounded by the sea. The pennies are Liberty's copper body. The wires are the parts that are made of iron. Would Liberty corrode so fast if she were made only of iron or only of copper?

Time On A Dime

Kitchen timers can be quite expensive. But you can make one for next to nothing. Make a three-minute timer to use while boiling eggs. If you follow these instructions, you'll end up with a device people used to measure time before they invented clocks!

You Will Need:
- pencil
- cone-shaped paper cup
- jar as wide as the cup
- sand
- watch with a second hand
- sheet of paper

Directions:

Study a grain of sand. Use a pencil to make a hole the same size inside your cup at the bottom.

Set the paper cup in a jar. Get ready to pour a little bit of sand into the cup. Wait for the second hand of your watch to strike twelve. The very second it does, pour sand and note the time it takes to fall on a sheet of paper.

Did it take less then three minutes? If so, add a little more sand. Once again, note the time it takes the sand to fall. Add the times up. If you have more than three minutes, pour some sand out. If you have less, add some sand.

Repeat the above steps until you have sand that falls in exactly three minutes. When you do, time it again just to be sure.

INDEX